"What if you could know

"Some like to read the last chapter of a book to see if they like how it ends before they commit to reading the rest of the book. It would be nice to do that with our lives as well—to use the ending as a catalyst for how we make decisions and approach life. In his book HOMESICK, Freddie Tyler opens a window to reveal the future through the lives of four characters.

"Freddie Tyler knows commitment and dedication becoming an Olympic champion, but more importantly, he decided his future for eternity and then began pouring his life into others as a committed husband, loving father, dedicated teacher, and talented coach. Now as an author, he speaks into our lives by masterfully unveiling a story that invites us to write our own.

"When you open the pages of this book, you will not be able to put it down until you discover and KNOW your future--the future you desire for your life. This powerful story grips the reader and speaks to each and every one of our lives no matter where our journey has led us to this point. Though the story is fiction, he invites us into the lives of these characters and a critical decision each has made that determines the course of their future.

"By introducing us to each of these characters, Freddie Tyler truly and clearly presents the options for each of us and the future that follows our decision—both for this life and eternity. We never know when our life on this earth will complete its last chapter—but, as this book wonderfully portrays, we will have decided where we will spend eternity, and we will know what that eternity looks like.

"Read this book, decide your future, and then surrender to let the story of your life be written one chapter at a time."

ERIC & WENDY HARBINSON

Missionaries in Nicaragua.

HOMESICK

Where Will You Call Home? The Choice Is Yours

FREDDIE TYLER

Storehouse Media Group, LLC
Jacksonville, Florida

HOMESICK: **Where Will You Call Home? The Choice Is Yours**

Copyright © 2018 by Freddie Tyler

Storehouse Media Group, LLC
Jacksonville, Florida
www.StorehouseMediaGroup.com
publish@StorehouseMediaGroup.com

Ordering Information:
Quantity sales. Special discounts are available with the Publisher at the email address above and type in subject line "Special Sales Department."

The views expressed in this work are solely those of the author(s) and do not necessarily reflect the views of the publisher, and the publisher hereby disclaims any responsibility for them.

Cover Photo by Renee Tyler

HOMESICK / Freddie Tyler —1st ed.

ISBN: 978-1-943106-24-0 (paperback)
ISBN: 978-1-943106-25-7 (ebook)

Library of Congress Control Number: 2017963964

Printed in the United States of America

DEDICATION

This is dedicated to the love of my life, my wife Renee,
who if not in my life, this book would have
not been written.

HOMESICK

Our body is like a house we live in here on earth. When it is destroyed, we know that God has another body for us in heaven. The new one will not be made by human hands as a house is made. This body will last forever.

Right now, we cry inside ourselves because we wish we could have our new body which we will have in heaven. We will not be without a body. We will live in a new body. While we are in this body, we cry inside ourselves because things are hard for us.

It is not that we want to die. Instead, we want to live in our new bodies. We want this dying body to be changed into a living body that lasts forever.

It is God Who has made us ready for this change. He has given us His Spirit to show us what He has for us (2 Corinthians 5: 1-5).

EPIGRAPH

"You must think of yourself – for God sent His Son into the world to save you!

"Here I insist that you must have some faith about yourself and I am almost afraid to say it because someone will send me a critical, nagging letter.

"I am not asking you to have faith in yourself – I am only insisting that it is right for you to show faith about yourself, faith in Christ and in what He has promised you as an individual person.

"That is, you must believe that you are the one He meant when He said, "Come home."

– Jesus: The Life and Ministry of God the Son--
Collected Insights
from A.W. Tozer

CONTENTS

Foreword   xiii

Acknowledgments   xv

Introduction   xvii

Prologue   Fall of Man   xix

Chapter 1   Sickness   1

Chapter 2   Terror   5

Chapter 3   Best Friends   9

Chapter 4   Attack   19

Chapter 5   Heaven   27

Chapter 6   Adultery   31

Chapter 7   Hell   51

Chapter 8   Unspeakable Joy   55

Chapter 9   Utter Darkness   67

Chapter 10   Peace on Earth   77

Chapter 11   Wheat & Tares   81

Chapter 12   In the Father's Presence   93

Chapter 13   Separation and a Second Chance   105

Chapter 14   Return to Earth   111

Chapter 15   "Yes, I AM Coming Soon"   121

Epilogue   Rapture and Tribulation   127

About the Author: Freddie Tyler   139

FOREWORD

It has been said that all of our lives are a story.

If you think about it, that statement really carries more truth than most individuals want to deal with. Because if our lives are indeed a story, then the question has to be asked of each of us – what kind of story are you telling with your life?

In *Homesick*, Freddie Tyler takes each of us as readers and pushes us into the lives and stories of some fascinating individuals. In these rich characters we find not only people we have met and know, but in some ways, we find ourselves. As their stories move forward, they pull us along and we begin to care and wonder what will happen to each of them...and of course, ultimately, what will happen to each of us.

It is always fascinating to find that a story about others is actually a story about ourselves. *Homesick* dares to pull back the curtain and suggest that the things we experience in life really are only a glimpse of what is most important and how we choose to live has a ripple effect today and throughout eternity.

Freddie Tyler has spent his life becoming and living like a champion. Now as an author, he once again shows his gold medal stroke, this time on a keyboard, as he weaves together a compelling narrative that submerges you in a world where every moment matters.

As you turn the page, get ready... a story awaits, and somewhere in it we all can find what we are homesick for.

JEFF DIXON
Transformational Architect, The Church @ 434
Author, *Dixon on Disney* series

ACKNOWLEDGMENTS

I am grateful to my wife Renee for how she loves me and challenges me to be a better man for Christ. Because of her love for Jesus and her understanding that our family needed to include Him, we embarked on a lifelong journey to seek the Kingdom of God and to live a life of love. She has lived that life of love much better than me. It was her love for Christ that showed me His love for me. Renee has given her life for me, for our children, for my sisters and brother, and for innumerable others who God has brought across her path. I am a better man because of the extraordinary woman she is.

I am grateful for my children and grandchildren because the love I have for them has helped me to understand God's love for me.

Thanks to Pastor Jeff Dixon (Dixon on Disney) for reading the manuscript, his personal writing tips and encouraging me to move forward with *Homesick*.

A special thank-you to Angela Rodriguez (author of *Blink* and *What are the Chances?*) for proof reading the manuscript, making grammatical and writing corrections, as well as suggestions for content, and for believing that this story is worth telling. Angela, your help was invaluable!

I am thankful to the LORD for the men He has put in my life to demonstrate His love, His peace, His kindness, and His joy. The humility these men have demonstrated in their lives has shown me how to be a better husband, father, brother, and friend.

INTRODUCTION

"Yet God has made everything beautiful for its own time. He has planted eternity in the human heart, but even so people cannot see the whole scope of God's work from beginning to end."
(Ecclesiastes 3:11)

Donovan Jordan and Wade Gallo are best friends and have been since elementary school. Their bond is on a level that is different from blood brothers. Carol Wallace and Bianca Vega have been friends for only half a dozen years and yet their connection to one another is also extraordinarily intimate.

Homesick is the story of the journeys these two men and two women take into the afterlife, into eternity. Donovan and Wade travel together as do Carol and Bianca. What they encounter in those journeys I hope will make you think about the journey you will one day take.

At some time in your life you have probably missed home, wherever that may have been. You went overnight to a friend's house, or to camp for a week, or maybe when you entered the military, or went off to college. It is quite possible you never had a physical place to call home to miss, and yet you still experienced homesickness. You missed not having a home and wondered what that would be like. This might be the worst homesickness of all.

The thought of dying is not something people regularly think about. You may think about death when a member of your family or a friend dies. We will push the thought of it out of our minds as quickly as possible when we have been confronted by the deaths of people in a terrorist attack or a catastrophic natural disaster such as an earthquake or hurricane. The truth of life is that it ends in death.

While not everyone has a building to call home, every man and woman have a home here on Earth called a body. This is where YOU reside. This home is also temporary. In spite of efforts to "repair" or "remodel," this home of ours will one day die. The good news is that when death comes, every man and woman have the opportunity to "move into" the most wonderful home imaginable when their earthly home is gone.

What will your home look like? Donovan, Wade, Carol, and Bianca will give you a glimpse of what it could look like. It is my hope and prayer that everyone who reads this story will be homesick, homesick for Heaven.

PROLOGUE

FALL OF MAN

"'Yes,' he told them, 'I saw Satan fall from
heaven like lightning!'"
(Luke 10:18)

The sky opens and an angelic being named Lucifer
tumbles down to earth. This beautiful being was
created by God to lead the worship of Heaven, to lead
the praises to the Creator of all things. Instead, this
creature decides he wants to be the one who is
worshipped and praised. It is a fatal choice.

When his coup fails, he is cast down out of Heaven
along with all the angels who chose to follow him. He
now devotes his entire existence into lashing out at
God. He is now referred to as Satan or the devil, and is
fully committed to the destruction of mankind. He
covets every man's soul, knowing each lost soul grieves
the Creator. Those he cannot persuade to deny God,

he and his minions work to discourage, to make ineffective for God's mission of redemption.

He has sealed his own fate but has determined to take as many souls as he can. It is this event, and this fallen angelic being, that has redirected the fate of mankind. God could have just vaporized Lucifer. Instead, God allowed him to live in order to allow the remaining angels to understand the concept of choice. They must choose to praise God for who he is and what he has done.

When a person understands how much God loves them, it will change their lives, now and for all eternity. It is the same choice He gives to mankind, receive his love or reject it.

Chapter One

SICKNESS

"By his wounds you are healed."
(1 Peter 2:24c)

Wade Gallo has been battling colon cancer for a year and a half. It appears the battle is almost over, and cancer will be the victor. Wade's wife Emily is anxious for his best friend Donovan to arrive at the hospital.

Donovan Jordan maneuvers his black Chevy Tahoe through the typically nightmarish Central Florida traffic and onto I-4. Semi-trucks, SUVs, sedans, and compact cars are packed bumper to bumper in all three lanes heading west. The rain is not helping. It is as if buckets of water are being poured from the sky. He turns up the radio to help drown out the hypnotic rhythm of the wipers going back and forth.

He knows the Tahoe he is driving is more practical than the Porsche he has always wanted. Donovan understands that with two boys, a small sports car is not going to cut it when it comes to loading up for a weekend camping trip or heading to the beach, especially when Lucas and Jacob include their friends.

He loves riding up high on the road but knows when it comes to parking, especially at the hospital or downtown, a small sports car is better suited to zip into a parking spot or out of it, not to mention this bumper-to-bumper traffic.

"I was hoping to be at the hospital half an hour ago!" laments Donovan. As he exits the interstate, he makes his way down Princeton Street to Orlando Baptist Hospital where he is stopped at yet another red light. Donovan knows Emily is desperate for him to get to the hospital, which only adds to his frustration.

Donovan's father was in Baptist Hospital a couple of years before while suffering from depression, so he is familiar with the hospital's layout, from the parking to the maze of corridors to the hospital gift shop and cafeteria. Getting to Wade's room wouldn't be a problem … he just has to get there. It will take another ten minutes until he reaches the hospital parking garage.

Wade Gallo is Donovan's best friend. Their friendship goes back to elementary school in Columbus, Indiana.

Donovan reminisces. *We are best friends having shared so much in life. It seems like yesterday when we celebrated winning the Indiana High School State Football Championship. I can still remember getting off the Columbus Cougars' bus at Purdue University's stadium in West Lafayette. Seeing the painted lines on the field and smelling the fresh-cut turf as well as the concession stands with hamburgers, hot dogs, popcorn, and pizza still linger after all these years.*

We won the game in the final two minutes when Wade caught a fifteen-yard pass from Jimmy Jones and ran thirty-five yards for the winning touchdown. The defending champion Lafayette Lions ran out of time after a "Hail Mary" pass into the end zone fell incomplete.

The Cougars' sideline and stands erupted into a raucous celebration as the game clock wound down to zero. Wade and I were hugging and jumping up and down as we joined in the jubilation. There will be no celebrating today.

This dreary February day only intensifies Donovan's depressed mood as he makes his way into the hospital parking garage. It's dark and has a musty smell from the dampness of the recent rain. The hospital is fifteen stories high with thousands of rooms filled with people in need of healing. Many like Wade are in a fight for their lives.

He is lying in bed. The colon cancer he has been fighting has metastasized to other parts of his body.

This insidious disease has brought him to death's door. The prognosis is dire, and a decision about hospice is imminent.

More thoughts of the life they have shared cascade through Donovan's mind.

We first met in Mrs. Bates' third-grade class at Lakemont Elementary School in Columbus. We were friends instantly. I can't explain why. We just connected. From that time on, we were inseparable.

The two of us always insisted on being on the same team for dodgeball, softball, football, capture the flag, kick the can, or any other game that was being played before school, after school, or at recess. We would spend the night at each other's houses. We made forts together, went fishing, and played army together. The Little League baseball championship we won when were twelve was the first of many other athletic successes we shared.

In high school, we were teammates on the football, basketball, and track teams. We were also college roommates and best men in each other's weddings as well.

Chapter Two

TERROR

"For as long as I can remember, I have felt
tormented and at war, and have felt hatred
and animosity for Americans."
(Osama Bin Laden)

In an abandoned warehouse four blocks from
Baptist Hospital, a group of men are busy loading
boxes and small crates into a white Ford van and a
black Chevrolet SUV. The contents of the crates are
automatic weapons, and in the boxes are
ammunition and explosives. There are also a variety
of electronic devices that are being put into the
SUV, along with several grenade launchers and two
hand-held missile launchers.

The five men loading the van appear to be of Middle Eastern descent. They all have short black hair and beards. Their pants, shirts, and jackets are generic, but they all have name-brand sports shoes on.

Two of the three men loading the SUV are also of Middle Eastern descent with black hair, but these two are clean-shaven. They are also dressed in nondescript clothing but are wearing leather shoes.

The third man is a stocky white man with shoulder-length dishwater blonde hair. This man also has a beard, but it is long and full. He is wearing jeans, T-shirt, and boots.

A cell phone rings, and the tallest of the Middle Eastern men loading the SUV checks his phone and answers it. After a brief conversation, he hangs up and barks orders to the other men. They quickly complete loading the guns and other equipment in to the vehicles and climb in themselves. The engines rev up, and the tires squeal. Smoke rises from the pavement as they race out of the parking lot and onto a side street that leads directly to Baptist Hospital.

The vehicles slow down and are completely unnoticed as they pull up outside of the hospital. The rain has slowed to a drizzle, the pavement is damp, and puddles of water are flowing down the gutters.

Two of the men step out of the SUV with no thought of the water streaming down the road, and they casually walk down the sidewalk. They appear to be looking for something or someone as they peer down the street and up at the hospital windows. The driver side door of the van opens.

One of the men jumps out. He quickly looks to his left and then his right before proceeding around the back of the van and across a grassy area to a door on the side of the building. He jiggles the door handle. He then reaches into his jacket pocket, takes out a key card, and slides it through the card reader. When he turns the handle this time, the door opens.

The man gives a thumbs-up to his comrade in the front passenger seat of the van.

Chapter Three

Best Friends

"So Jonathan made a solemn pact with David,
saying, 'May the Lord Destroy all your
enemies!' And Jonathan made David reaffirm
his vow of friendship again, for Jonathan loved
David as he loved himself."
(1 Samuel 20:16-17)

Donovan strides down the hospital corridor. At six feet four inches and two hundred twenty-five pounds of muscle, he is an imposing figure. He is tan, has the blonde hair of a young California surfer, and bright emerald eyes.

Doctors and nurses sit at computers in the nurse's station or are standing flipping through papers attached to clipboards, the grimaces on their faces expressing the seriousness of their work. There are several patients dawdling along in the hallway, hooked up to machines which monitor their vitals. Their continuous beeping and blinking lights are almost like a symphony, fit only for a place like this.

Hospitals can be depressing, but at Baptist Hospital, the rooms and hallways are painted in cheerful colors coordinated in a way that is almost heavenly. The hallways are infused with life instead of dead overtones normally associated with hospital corridors. The pictures and paintings lining the walls are inspiring, fun, and encouraging. It is clean yet not antiseptic. It breaks the mold of a typical hospital.

Donovan peers into some of the rooms as he passes by. Patients are sitting in chairs while others are lying back on their beds. Many have no expression on their faces, only a blank stare. Some watch television while others chat with visitors. He hears several patients telling whoever will listen that they just want to go home. They want to sleep in their own beds, eat at their own dinner tables, and shower in their own bathrooms. Other patients are on gurneys and being wheeled down the hallway on their way to surgery or are being taken for more testing.

Most of the patients on this floor are older, in their sixties and up. A few on this floor are around Wade's age, in their thirties or forties. He watches their faces and dreads not only the reality of Wade's situation but that he will have to face his wife Emily. He wishes his own wife Judith was here. She is so much better at these things than he is. Judith is like an angel. There are no words that will make this better.

Donovan greets a nurse just outside the room, knocks, peeks in, and greets Emily, Wade, and their two girls Layla and Sophia. He gives Emily and the girls a hug and takes hold of Wade's left hand with both of his as if to say, "I'm here for you."

The expressions on Emily's, Layla's, and Sophia's faces tell the story of Wade's condition. The tears welling up in their eyes reveal the fact that he has taken a turn for the worse. Wade recognizes his old friend, mumbles a greeting, and gives him a faint smile, too weak to do any more.

This is not the same man Donovan once knew. His handsome coffee complexion is now so very pale, and he has lost his hair, which at times had been in long dreads. His strong limbs have atrophied to half their size, his eyes are sunken and dull, not the sparkling and vibrant brown that once made the ladies swoon.

Talking directly to Donovan, Wade's eyes slowly close as he speaks in a hushed voice. "I just want it to be over. I want it to end so I can be in my Father's house. God's house will be so spectacular. The way life is right now makes me long for Jesus and for Heaven where there is no more pain."

Donovan prays silently, "Lord, please give us a miracle."

With his eyes still closed, Wade begins to remember his own life and how blessed he has been. He recalls his friendship with Donovan being very meaningful because of how the Jordan family had treated him and his family.

As one of the few black students at Lakemont Elementary, that never seemed to be an issue with the Jordans. To them, he was just Wade Gallo. They were all very supportive as he pursued his athletic career. The entire community rallied around him.

His mother and father were very involved in a local non-denominational church, The Word of Grace. He was aware early on of the athletic gift the Lord had given him. He never had a problem outrunning or outjumping any of his classmates. He could throw a ball farther than any of them. The other kids could never make catching a ball on the run look as easy as him either. He was above average as a student, but his passion was sports, and he loved Jesus and the Word of God. He could still remember the big games and the championships.

But what he remembers best was meeting Emily at Indiana University. It was his senior year, and he was an NFL prospect, projected to go in the second or third round. Eventually he ended up with the Seattle Seahawks in the second round.

Emily was a sophomore and beautiful. She was not as impressed with him as he was with himself. It took a lot of convincing for her to agree to a first date. What he found in this beautiful lady was a woman with a heart for God. She was just what he needed to keep him grounded.

"What is the latest report?" Donovan asks Emily.

She replies, "They've told us to contact hospice. He doesn't have much time left."

She has already taken time off from her job as a paralegal with Barks and Barks to care for Wade. Emily then tells Donovan she is going to take the girls down to the cafeteria to get a snack. With the end near, she wants to give these two friends some final time together. She is sure Donovan will be able to lift Wade's spirits.

Donovan glances at Wade's daughters. They too are in elementary school like his sons and are another reminder of how long Wade and him have been friends. They met in the third grade, and even then, it was obvious that Wade was a gifted athlete. Donovan was an above-average athlete, but he considered himself the smarter of the two academically. He may have been too smart for his own good as he found himself in a lot of "hot water." Wade did not. While Donovan was pushing the envelope on all the rules, Wade was turning the pages of the Bible.

In college, unlike when they were young, Wade and Donovan were no longer inseparable. Donovan often found himself making choices he later regretted. Under pressure, he sometimes found a way to cheat in order to keep his grades up. He admits he was lazy. While being associated with Wade helped him win some degree of social acceptance, he often compromised what he knew to be right in order to be accepted on what he considered his own merits.

Donovan's life changed during his second tour in the Marines. That's when he met Judith. He was smitten immediately by her grace and her wonderfully sweet and confident spirit. Judith is "drop-dead gorgeous." Be assured, though, that she was also tough with a capital "T."

She was in her first tour of duty and was in a unit that was preparing to go to Afghanistan. Donovan's unit had just returned from the Middle East. At first, they emailed and texted each other. Eventually, they called or video chatted whenever the opportunity arose. That was so special because not only could Donovan hear her lyrical voice, he could see her incredibly beautiful face.

Judith did not re-enlist when her time was up and was honorably discharged. She had hoped to serve a second tour, but when her father passed away and her mother became ill, she knew she was needed at home. This was very attractive to Donovan. He loved his folks and family, but he was in this life to serve his own best interests. This woman taught him to look outside of himself, to love people. He didn't know how to do that, even though his mom and dad had been great role models of loving others, especially family and friends.

Judith knew he needed to get involved in a church that taught about the extravagant grace of Jesus. A year later, they ended up getting married and moved to Florida. Not long after that, Wade and Emily moved to Orlando too.

Chapter Four

THE ATTACK

"Tora, Tora, Tora!"
***(Words used by the Japanese military after
the bombing of Pearl Harbor. It means
surprise, lightning attack.)***

Moments after Emily and the girls leave, gunfire can be heard downstairs, and there is an explosion. This jars Donovan out of his recollections of the past and back to the present. The building rocks violently as if jolted by an earthquake.

There are two more explosions. The thunderous roar sounds like an EF-five tornado hitting the hospital. Pieces of concrete and glass rain down on the grass and sidewalk. Together the blasts seem to be both above and below them. It is a sudden reminder of the sounds of the war in that faraway desert.

Before Donovan can get his thoughts together, the room explodes. Hand-held missile launchers are being used by terrorists firing on the hospital. The next missile hits the wall outside of Wade's room with a violent boom, and he is catapulted out of his bed and onto the floor.

Donovan has been hurled five feet in to the air and lands on a machine that was once beside the bed. Part of the metal frame of the window has impaled him on his right side. He grimaces in pain as his eyes try to focus.

As he searches for Wade, Donovan feels the life force exiting his body. Shrapnel flies in every direction, as does the debris from the walls, ceiling, and windows. Shards of glass from the blown-out windows fly furiously around the room.

Wade's IV's and tubes have been ripped out of his arms and the oxygen tubes from his nose. He is now unconscious on the floor next to the door, debris from the shattered windows and walls covering him. The dust from the walls and ceiling tiles is thick in the air, and blood from Donovan's limp body pools on the floor beneath him.

Emily and the girls had just stepped off the elevator on the first floor on the opposite side of the hospital where the attack was taking place. The reverberation of the exploding missiles shook the ground underneath them. They instinctively duck down and then bend halfway up and are running toward the emergency exit.

Hospital staff, visitors, and ambulatory patients join the frenzied race to get out of the building. They are directed out the emergency exit to a grassy area directly in front of the hospital. This was typical operating procedure for a fire or bomb threat. Although it made sense for them to get out of the building, doing so was problematic with an active shooter.

The unexpected scenario was a direct attack on the hospital. Bomb scares and active gunmen were one thing, but this was just plain crazy!

Gunfire from automatic weapons could be heard, as well as the sound of the missiles exploding against the walls of the hospital. They could feel the building shaking in response.

Emily and the girls look up at the building, smoke billowing from the roof. They could not know the devastation the missiles had caused to the other side of the building.

It didn't take long for news of what was happening to reach them as others poured out of the building and into the area where they were standing. Emily checked to insure Layla and Sophia were okay. Both nodded their heads to affirm they were.

Layla asks in a soft voice, tears again welling up in her eyes, "Mommy, is Daddy okay?"

"Yes, I'm sure he's just fine," replies Emily, trying to sound confident for her girls, yet still wondering if what she said was true and how safe they were out in the open.

In a matter of just a few minutes, the attack had stopped. Sporadic gunfire could still be heard. It didn't take these fiends much time to wreak havoc on the patients, staff, visitors, and the building. There was always only one objective in attacks like this – kill as many people as possible!

The police and fire departments' responses are almost immediate as they begin arriving on the scene. The smoke on Wade's floor is very thick, and fires have consumed the majority of it.

The first responders and other rescue workers inside are working frantically to fight the blaze and find survivors, their fire-resistant coveralls, helmets, and masks hindering their movement and vision.

Outside, law enforcement is trying to secure the hospital and the surrounding area. The loud, regular popping of gunfire can now be heard as the police continue the gun battle they are engaged in with the men from the white van and the black SUV.

Two terrorists with missile launchers have been separated from the others, yelling to each other in an indistinguishable Arabic dialect. The van and SUV are trying to move down the street but are blocked by cars that have been abandoned by frightened bystanders.

Both terrorist vehicles, tires screeching, jump the curb, knocking down parking meters. They continue past the sidewalk and onto the grass, tearing it up as they mow down various bushes and flowers. People frantically dive behind walls or between abandoned cars to get out of the way.

Several police cars, including a tactical vehicle, block the terrorists in, and the sound of bullets riddling their vehicles pierces the air. The SUV explodes as bombs inside are detonated. Cars near the SUV also erupt into flames.

The driver of the van and the man with the longer hair in the front passenger seat are hit by a hail of bullets. The side doors open, and a third man falls out onto the ground.

One of the two men with missile launchers has been mortally wounded while the other man now lies on the pavement. It is difficult to determine if he is dead or not, though he is definitely not moving. Orlando police officers move in, sweep his weapon away, ensuring that he has no other weapons or a bomb vest.

Firemen and EMTs enter Wade's room, their eyes darting from one side of the room to the other. They see the two men unconscious on the floor. Their pulses are very weak and both men are bleeding from a variety of wounds to their heads, arms, legs, and torsos. The metal window frame is bent, still protruding from Donovan's chest. The pools and smears of their crimson blood make it difficult to determine how serious any of the other wounds are.

The EMTs work hard to help stabilize the two victims and wonder where they take victims of an attack on a hospital.

Answering their unspoken question, a voice on the radio directs them to Northside Hospital, fifteen miles away. There are no other facilities closer.

Chapter Five

HEAVEN

"Don't let your hearts be troubled. Trust in
God, and trust also in me. There is more than
enough room in my Father's home."
(John 14:1)

Donovan and Wade walk side by side. It's tough to determine if they are walking down a road, a path, or possibly a brightly illuminated tunnel.

They recognize each other but cannot distinguish anything other than the blinding white light around them. Both are disoriented, and neither has yet to acknowledge that Wade is walking alongside Donovan with no difficulty when just moments earlier he was bedridden and dying.

Wade inquires, "Where are we?"

Donovan replies, "I'm not sure where we are, but I'm sure neither of us has been here before."

"What happened? How is it I'm walking and feeling no pain?" He is now aware that just a few minutes ago, he was in a hospital bed, dying.

"I would say we are dead, but I've never heard of a story where TWO people are dead together," Donovan responded.

They move toward a light, even brighter than the one all around them. The sound of their own footsteps is all they hear. They sense that they're not alone.

An angel greets them. He is an imposing figure. The two men draw back.

The angel says to them, "You have nothing to fear." His face is glowing, and his smile is gentle and sweet. He informs them that he will be their guide.

It is inexplicable. Donovan is still trying to wrap his mind around this miracle. Wade looks completely normal, healthy, and strong. He stretches his arms, flexes the muscles of his hands, and rubs his legs, completely bewildered at what has happened and where he is.

Donovan and Wade have arrived in Heaven at the same time, experiencing the same memories of being in the hospital, the explosions, and now being here together.

This is unprecedented. This has to be a dream, but people don't dream the same dream at the same time either.

What is going on?

Chapter Six

ADULTERY

"Thou shalt not commit adultery."
(Exodus 20:14)

Part I - Betrayal

Carol Wallace exits Room 415 at the Regal Hotel. She adjusts her short black dress, turns, and kisses her lover goodbye. He brushes her long blonde hair back, gazes into her sparkling blue eyes, and kisses her again.

As she turns away, he reaches for her hand in a desperate attempt to draw her back into the room. Who wouldn't want this gorgeous woman to come back into his arms? She is tall at five-foot-eleven and captivatingly beautiful with vibrant blue eyes and soft, tan skin. Her fit, curvaceous body completes this irresistible package.

The Regal is the finest hotel in San Antonio. No expense was spared in the design, building, and furnishing of the hotel. Each suite has a completely stocked kitchen area, plush furniture, expensive artwork, Jacuzzi, seventy-five-inch flat-screen television, stereo system, and king-size bed with silk sheets.

As she steps into the elevator, Carol takes out her cell phone to call her office. She wants to confirm several appointments she has for the next day and to ensure she has RSVP'd for the San Antonio Area Real Estate Awards Banquet. She is up for Realtor of the Year, and her company is in the running for Real Estate Company of the Year. Carol has made over two million dollars in the last two years.

Her focus changes after the receptionist informs her that Sam had stopped by earlier.

Sam is Carol's husband. She knows her clothes have the smell of her lover's cologne, so she will have to put this dress, as well as the rest of her clothes, in the washer immediately. She begins to spin another tale in her mind to tell Sam.

Carol and Sam have been married for eight years. She loves Sam, whatever that really means. At least that's what she tells people. Maybe she is trying to convince herself she still loves him. He's just not enough for her. It's not that Sam is unattractive. In fact, he is a very handsome man who takes pride in his physical appearance. His work is physically demanding, and yet Sam works out at the gym four or five times a week. The ladies definitely watch this six-foot-two specimen, hoping maybe he'll notice them.

While he enjoys the attention, Sam is serious about his vows to Carol. *It was fun in the beginning,* she thinks, *but now Sam is too serious, too calculating, and too exact. He is boring.* Carol is a free spirit, fun-loving, and her business success has seemingly come too easy. She receives a lot of attention from the various men she does business with: real-estate agents, mortgage brokers, attorneys, and other business associates.

Sam has not been so successful, and Carol has not made it easy on his male ego. She constantly belittles him in front of others and diminishes his job. He is so blue collar. Sam has his own business as well, working as a handyman. He can fix anything this side of the space shuttle, which ironically, was one of the things Carol used to love about him.

Sam does well enough, able to keep a steady flow of jobs coming in, including work Carol sends his way on the various properties she sells and manages. Unfortunately, he has not been able to bring in enough big jobs for him to hire some permanent employees and expand.

For Sam, life seems to be passing him by. He puts in long hours and is usually dead tired when he gets home. He and Carol rarely have time for each other, and he is well-aware of how attractive she is to other men.

Life has not always been like this for Carol. She remembers growing up in Nebraska, in a home filled with abuse and disappointment. Her family was a lower-middle-income family. Both her mom and dad worked dead-end jobs. They barely made enough money to pay the rent and put food on the table. She swore her life would be different.

Carol's father was very demeaning to her mother, constantly belittling her for the way she looked, how she cooked, and how she took care of the house and the kids. He was not too kind to Carol or her younger brother and sister either. Everyone was a burden to him. Their family never took a vacation, the kids always wore secondhand clothes, and friends were not a part of growing up in her house.

Carol decided very early on that she would do whatever it took to get out of that house and as far away as she could. During the time when she had no choice but to stay, she managed to escape through drug use, alcohol, and sex. In all reality, even though her life now seemed better, she continues to use drugs, alcohol, and sex as a coping mechanism. Emptiness consumes her heart.

Carol's best friend Bianca Vega suggested she check out a program that she had heard about called Celebrate Recovery, where men and women find healing through trusting Jesus Christ and learn how to overcome their addictions. Bianca had a couple of friends who had gone through the program, and it had changed their lives. She was envious of how they spoke of Jesus as though he was a personal friend.

Carol would deflect that suggestion, saying she didn't have the time to get involved in a program like that. And besides, this Jesus didn't seem so real to her. "How can someone I can't see give me the fulfillment I need?" Carol would ask. She knew Bianca meant well and that she loved her, but she felt she could deal with it herself.

As she continues to review her life, she remembers the time she witnessed her father practically beat her mother to death. It was so scary. They were like two animals battling, and her mother finally collapsed onto the floor when her father hit her on the side of her head with a lamp. Carol tries not to remember the vacant look in her mother's eyes as she lay there motionless.

She knew at that moment she would never let a man do that to her. No man would ever control her like that. This is why she had been so driven to succeed in business. She wanted control. Even in her affairs, she is in control. She meets her lovers when and where SHE decides.

Carol heads to the front of the hotel where her car is waiting. She tips the valet a hundred-dollar bill and jumps into her brand-new midnight-black Mercedes convertible. The young valet smiles and follows her with lust-filled eyes. She pulls out of the hotel parking lot, the tires squealing slightly as she presses firmly onto the gas pedal.

She dials Bianca's number. Bianca is the manager of a high-end fashion boutique. Carol has been trying to convince her to come to work with her in real estate. She knows Bianca would kill it in that business. Bianca is on the way to Carol's house to talk. She has her own share of issues to be resolved.

On the ride home, Carol continues to piece together the deceptive story she will tell Sam about where she has been and what she has been doing. She's pretty sure Sam never believes her, and she is uncertain why she takes the time to think up new lies.

She pulls into her garage, turns the engine off, and walks into the kitchen. Celeste, the housekeeper, has brewed a fresh pot of coffee before she left for the day. The rich smell of the finest Colombian brew wafts through the air.

Carol pours out two cups as her mind races through the past three years. Just the smell of this wonderful coffee is enough to perk her up.

While she has been successful in her business, the rest of her life is in shambles. Her marriage is a disaster, and she knows it's her fault. Her relationship with her daughter Suzie isn't much better since she spends precious little time with her. The success of her business has not been good for Carol, distracting her from her family and bringing irresistible temptations, and it's been terrible for Sam and Suzie. Sam has never been anything but a loving husband and certainly does not deserve the treatment she has given him.

Sam has always been supportive of her business and encouraging to her, despite his own failure to succeed in her eyes. The men she has hooked up with are nowhere near the man Sam is, and yet she continues to have affairs. Once, she actually had cheated on Sam with two different men at the same time.

Part II - Snapped

Sam is at the shooting range. The attendant notices he is agitated. He alternates between his handgun and his rifle, all the while muttering to himself about Carol's unfaithfulness, about how he loves her, about how poorly she treats him and their daughter.

The targets he is shooting at are all silhouettes of women. Sam targets the head, and then the sound of the gun firing, *pop, pop, pop* erupts. It is the same as he aims at the torso, the head, and finally the private areas--*pop, pop, pop*. There is a clacking sound as the shells bounce off the concrete floor.

Twice now, the attendants have asked him not to scream while shooting.

Everyone at the range is required to wear ear protectors because of the tremendous noise of gunfire, but they also keep them from understanding Sam's ranting. They are aware of his volatile behavior as he jumps up and down, shakes his fist, and leans his head back, screaming in delight and anguish at filling the targets with holes.

Finally, the range staff tells Sam to leave. He doesn't resist. He is now ready for his mission, and it is time to complete it.

The range personnel have no idea of what's going on in Sam's head. They are just glad to get him off the range and off the property. They contemplate contacting the police but decide not to. It's a critical mistake on their part.

Bianca opens the front door, shouts hello, and walks in. She has the posture and sultry walk of a supermodel, along with a smile so bright it lights up the room.

Carol invites her into the living room. Bianca has taken off her shoes and her feet delight at the touch of the plush carpet. The décor is elegant. All of the furniture is top of the line. Everything is perfectly coordinated, from the color of the walls to the fabric used in the furniture. Carol's entire house could be a model home, which is exactly what she intended as she often entertains clients.

Two cups of coffee sit on the coffee table. It's easy to fix Bianca's, lots of French Vanilla, and she is good to go. Carol and Bianca sit on the couch talking when Sam enters the room brandishing an AR-15 assault rifle. He also has a Glock 19 tucked into his waistband.

He barely looks like himself. His face is contorted into a frightening countenance. "I can't take your cheating anymore!" he screams.

He continues yelling at Carol about her infidelity, her selfishness and greed. Carol starts to stand up, but he screams at her to sit down. She quickly obeys and tries to get him to calm down.

Bianca reaches over and takes Carol's hand. The two women shrink back into the couch. They are both shaking in fear, their eyes are shut tight, and their teeth are clenched as Sam continues to rant.

Surely Sam won't hurt us, Bianca thinks. She wants to say something to Sam but can't find the words.

Sam exclaims, "I'm not going to put up with your lies and cheating anymore. I don't deserve this!" He continues screaming, "How could you do this to Suzie and me?"

He aims the gun at his wife and fires, emptying the clip. Carol shakes like a rag doll as the bullets tear through her body. There is an expression of horror frozen on her face.

Bianca leaps in between Carol and the barrage of lead now piercing her flesh. It is a mistaken effort to protect. Bianca thought she might be able to get both of them out of the path of the bullets, but they came too fast. The bullets tear through her and into Carol.

Blood, fabric from her dress, and flesh from her body spray everywhere. The smell of gunpowder is thick in the air. Her body is in shock from the wounds the bullets have inflicted.

She falls on top of Carol, who is bleeding so profusely the sofa cushions are now soaked. Bianca can hear that Carol's breathing is shallow, and her pulse is almost undetectable.

Bianca feels like she is floating. She is somehow above the tragic scene, and yet the smell of gunpowder and blood are palpable. Besides being stained a deep crimson, the couch is shredded. Other pieces of furniture, pictures, and various knick-knacks have been shattered by bullets. Glass and wood fragments are everywhere, along with deep-red blood spatter.

Bianca considers her own life. What will Marcos, her fiancé, think about this? He loves her so much, she knows that. How could her life end this way? She had so much to live for.

As horrible as this was, Bianca could never anticipate what was coming next.

She remembers growing up in Miami. She loved the sunny, warm climate of South Florida. The palm-lined beaches were beautiful, and the Hispanic culture of her ancestors permeated the city. Her grandparents on both sides came to America from Cuba before

Castro's Revolution. Her mother and father both grew up in Miami, but they continued to embrace their Cuban heritage and the Spanish language.

Bianca grew up in the Catholic Church. She vividly remembers the pageantry of the Christmas and Easter services. The priests looked so regal in their beautiful, elegant robes and with their crucifixes around their necks. She could still smell the incense. Almost everyone she knew was Catholic. She even remembers when the Pope came to Miami. Talk about pomp and circumstance. It was a grandiose celebration!

As a Catholic, she knew she had to behave and follow the rules. Her parents worked seven days a week, and as a result, they were not regular churchgoers. Her mother often went to confession and an occasional Mass, but they never missed Christmas and Easter.

Bianca was a good student in school. She had dreams of modeling and participated in local beauty pageants with the hope of one day becoming Miss America.

She is a statuesque brunette with the most beautiful brown complexion. Her eyes are a piercing dark brown that seem to dance inside her head. Her full lips are rarely without a red shade of lipstick, and her nose is perfect. All of it is framed by her shoulder-length brown hair.

Bianca also remembers being a fair athlete. She was a pretty good competitive swimmer but loved playing water polo. Unfortunately, she did not have the killer instinct necessary to be successful in any of these endeavors.

Bianca loves fashion and sports equally, and it was in both that she found her niche working for FASHLETIC, the perfect combination of fashion and athletics. A degree in marketing and finance from the University of Miami was a given for her.

The store Bianca manages in the Sun & Palms Mall is where she met her fiancé Marcos Bravo. Marcos is a sales representative for a national tool company that sells to House Depot in the mall. Her body is shutting down, and she is no longer cognizant of her surroundings or condition.

Carol and Bianca are both still, and yet their eyes are wide open, their faces white as ghosts. It is a gruesome scene. Breathing heavily, Sam backs out of the room, tears filling his eyes as he turns to run out the back door. A neighbor has called 911, reporting hearing shots fired at the Wallace residence.

Sirens wail in the background, getting louder as the police roll into the driveway and onto the front lawn. EMTs are not far behind, but no one enters the residence until the half dozen police are sure the perpetrator is no longer in the house, and the threat of danger is over.

Neighbors gather in front of Sam and Carol's house. They heard the gunfire and sense that something horrible has taken place. One of those neighbors is George Stevens.

The police arrive and surround the house, and several enter. They can be heard calling out to each other as they clear each room.

Those searching the outer perimeter have established it is secure. After several more minutes, confirmation comes that the inside of the house is also secure.

One of the police officers appears at the front door. He signals the EMTs that it's safe to go in.

Two ambulances back up to the front door. Several minutes later, the EMTs are pushing two stretchers out the door toward them. They can be overheard talking to each other as well as talking into their radios. They bring two women out and take them to Grace Medical.

They then advise the Grace Medical E.R. that they have two gunshot victims. Another several minutes passes before the ambulances scream out of the driveway with their sirens blaring and lights flashing.

George is a friend of Sam and Carol as well as Bianca and Marcos. He recognizes Bianca's car in the

Wallace's driveway so he calls Marcos. He knows Marcos' number since they play in the same basketball league and occasionally get together for pick-up games on Saturday mornings. George and his wife Cherie had originally met Marcos and Bianca at the Wallace's and immediately clicked with them.

When George tells Marcos what happened at the Wallace's, Marcos drops his cell phone and George can hear him screaming.

After several minutes, he comes back on the phone sobbing. "Is she okay, George? Is she okay?"

"All I can tell you is that they have taken her to Grace Medical Hospital," replies George.

Marcos immediately sprints to his car and rushes to Grace Medical. It seems as if his BMW 430i never hits the pavement as he races through city traffic, weaving back and forth between the myriad of cars, trucks, and motorcycles.

Marcos bursts through the doors of the emergency room and makes an inquiry about Bianca's condition.

From the grim look on the medical staff's faces, he knows it's bad. They inform him she is in surgery, and her condition is very serious. When he asks about Carol, they tell him she died while being transported to the hospital.

This just doesn't make sense, Marcos thinks. *How could Sam have done this, and why was Bianca shot? We knew things weren't great between Carol and Sam, but I never thought he would come unhinged like this.*

Marcos overhears the EMTs and police officers talking about the gruesomeness of the crime scene, and he becomes sick to his stomach. His face has gone sheet white, the news draining every bit of blood from it.

He immediately darts into the nearest men's room.

Chapter Seven

HELL

"They will be punished with eternal
destruction, forever separated from the Lord
and his glorious power."
(2 Thessalonians 1:9)

Carol and Bianca are in a dark tunnel. A musty odor
becomes increasingly rancid. The smell of death is
unmistakable, even to these women who have never
been connected to death.

There is a sense of foreboding as the temperature
continues to rise. The darkness is so thick you can feel
it. The sounds are nearly incomprehensible. The
volume seems to increase and decrease. Screaming,
yelling, shouts of anguish, and screeching. It's

terrifying. The origin of the sounds is difficult to decipher. Are they animal or human sounds?

While the tunnel is dark, Carol and Bianca are somehow able to distinguish each other, if barely. They are trying to figure out what has happened and where they are, unsure if they are alive or dead. Is it all just a horrible nightmare?

Just as with Donovan and Wade, Carol and Bianca know shared death experiences are unheard of, and yet they begin to realize they have died together.

Both women feel nauseous. The smells assaulting their noses are so putrid they are feeling sicker and sicker.

The pitch blackness they are fumbling through is disorienting. They can barely determine if they are right side up or upside down as they feel like they are spinning on some maniacal carnival ride, making them dizzy.

The unhuman screams are becoming louder and more distinct. It sounds like weeping and gnashing of teeth, both with sorrow and anger. They can feel the pain and the anger of the lost souls.

Carol reaches out to Bianca, trying to find her hand. *This is horrific. What is this place?* Carol thinks, as she clenches her teeth in anguish.

Chapter Eight

UNSPEAKABLE JOY

"I tell you that in the same way there will be
more rejoicing in Heaven over one sinner who
repents than over ninety-nine righteous persons
who do not need to repent."
(Luke 15:7)

Two men and two women, close friends, die in brutally intimate and horrific circumstances.

"How is it the two of us have arrived in Heaven at exactly the same time?" Donovan asks.

Wade replies, "I have no idea." He pauses before continuing. "Do you feel it, Donovan? Do you feel the peace and joy, the absolute bliss of this place? I'm beginning to understand the concept of shalom, being whole and complete."

They are now close to the end of the tunnel. Wade says, "I've always wondered what heaven would be like, Donovan, and now I think we're about to find out."

As they exit the tunnel, they see a group of people. They are standing just outside an ornate wall with an enormous pearl gate. There are a total of twelve gates.

The wall, which is made of jasper, doesn't appear to be in place to defend what is on the other side. It is simply a beautiful structure. The street inside the gate is gold, but the purity of the gold makes it practically transparent.

Upon closer inspection, they discover these people are family members and friends who had died, some of them a long time ago. Donovan's grandfather Joseph, known as "Papa Joe," is here, as well as Wade's mother Emma. The sweet, delighted expression on her face as she catches Wade's attention is so lovely.

His face is an expression of unadulterated love as his smile consumes it, and he embraces her. There are also aunts, uncles, and friends from school, church, and work.

One after another greets and welcomes them to eternity. Each person has a youthful appearance, no signs of age, and the expression on each of their faces is a smile that defines the occasion: joyous! These souls have come to greet them and begin a celebration in Heaven that is repeated over and over as men and women pass from mortal life to eternal life.

Many of the relatives they meet they never knew on Earth, yet they know they are family. There is an incredible feeling of total acceptance and the joy of togetherness.

Donovan's favorite aunt, Sara, is among those welcoming him to Heaven. She is full of life. The wavy, brown hair of her youth and soft vibrant complexion have returned. "You'll love it here, Donovan," she says with a gentle, loving voice. Her face seems to shine, as do the others who have greeted them.

Aunt Sara continues, "It is really nothing like we imagined it would be when we were on Earth. There are no harps and clouds, no all-day gatherings of singing *Hallelujah*. Heaven is FUN! Our Father is fun! The LORD invented all of the fun things we do.

You will see people in dozens of activities like being outdoors, studying, enjoying fellowship, singing, reading, dancing, creating art, playing, or working. Work here is the way it was in the Garden of Eden. It is a joy, not a burden.

We are always active, but we never get tired, sweat, or get out of breath. You'll notice no one wears glasses, has braces, uses crutches, or even has a need for bandages. We are spirit beings in perfected bodies. Isn't it glorious?!"

"It certainly is Aunt Sara, but how long have I been dead?" asks Donovan.

"Here in Heaven, there are no longer hours, days, weeks, or months," Aunt Sara replies. "There is just eternity. Back on Earth, time is so oppressive, but here in Heaven, there is no hurrying or urgency about anything. On Earth, time seemed to either take forever or went by too quickly. That is not the case here in Heaven. We are never bored since everything we do is giving glory to the LORD."

As they move through the pearl gate, Donovan's and Wade's eyes search back and forth, their heads moving left and right.

They see a burly man with a beard. Donovan looks at Wade and exclaims, "That's Abraham!"

"I know!" answers Wade.

"How could we possibly have known that?" asks Donovan.

"I don't know. I just knew it. There's King David!" Wade responds.

"I can't explain it either," says Donovan, "It's as if we have known them forever and would have recognized them anywhere."

The prophet Daniel and two of the twelve disciples, Peter and John, are there as well. By their expressions and hand gestures, they seem to be having a very lively discussion.

David is not dressed as a king. None of the others are clothed in garments from their time on Earth. They wear robes just like the Bible says in Revelation. These robes are not like the ones from Hollywood movies; they have a universally majestic sense to them, each having been dipped in the blood of Jesus. Righteousness covers everyone wearing these robes.

At the same time, they are completely individual. They are the same, but different. It is truly wondrous.

In Heaven, people are casually talking to one another. Mostly, you just seem to know who they are, or their name at least. Likewise, the people they observe are talking to every person like an old friend, their body language expressing how relaxed they are with one another. They discuss their lives on Earth and a myriad of other topics.

Now only feet away, Donovan spots two men. The first they recognize to be Jesus. The indescribable glory that surrounds Him is the giveaway.

They ask David who the second man is. David tells them it is Adam. He is tall, handsome, and looks to be in perfect physical shape. Jesus has his arm around Adam, and they are laughing.

As Jesus makes eye contact with Donovan and Wade, He comes over to them. He hugs them and says, "Welcome home!"

He looks directly into Donovan's eyes. His eyes are so loving and soft, certainly not the "blazing eyes" of Revelation.

Donovan feels him "looking" right in to his heart, and yet he has no sense of guilt or shame, only peace and joy. He is reminded of Psalm 139, "Search me O' God and know my heart…"

And it is obvious He does. The LORD continues to smile that sweet, sweet smile. "The Father is expecting you. He is quite excited to see the two of you!" Jesus exclaims.

Donovan and Wade have the exact same thought: *Whoa! We have just met our Lord face to face. He hugs and welcomes us, and then tells us that the Lord God Almighty, the Creator of all things, not only wants to see us, but He is EXCITED to see us.*

As Jesus leaves, He casually tells them, "We'll see you in the throne room. You'll be overwhelmed by its beauty; you'll love it."

They hear a sound all around that is soothing, comforting, and peaceful. It calms their souls.

The smells they experience are delightful. The fragrance of flowers, the smell of fresh-baked cookies, and then it is the mist of the ocean. There is nothing they can compare it to.

The trees, mountains, grass, and flowers are beyond the perfection of anything they have seen on earth. The shades of green seem to be endless. Each leaf and blade of grass is uniquely different. The grass is perfectly manicured. It is all perfect, but not in a "cookie cutter" kind of way.

There is randomness, but even the randomness is perfect. The rivers and lakes shimmer with a beauty beyond comprehension. No shadow is cast. The sun is absent, and there aren't any stars. Only the light of God is present.

Children play happily in the fields. Men and women can be seen all around, involved in a variety of activities and pursuits.

No one coughs or sneezes. Everyone is so filled with energy and vitality.

Dogs, cats, foxes, lions, lambs, tigers, bears, and any animal you can imagine are walking, running, or stretched out looking so relaxed. There is harmony among them. The dogs bark and run playfully through the grass. Birds of many varieties and colors fill the sky. You can hear the birds in the trees chirping cheerfully, and it is a grand sound.

You look into the distance, and it is at the same time infinite and close. This is Heaven.

Wade and Donovan's angelic escort asks if they would like something to drink. The answer is yes, and they are treated to "living water." It is the most refreshing drink they have ever tasted.

They were also given food. The food was an avalanche of pleasure for their taste buds, an epicurean's delight. The flavors could not be described with earthly terms.

They walk along a street of gold, pure like the one they walked on as they passed through the pearl gate. The vastness of heaven is mind-blowing. It is not possible to distinguish the beginning and the end. Everything is seamless. Their earthly sense of balance is tested because of this.

Their guide assures them they will adjust. Their presence is different than those around them since they have not fully transitioned to eternal life.

The street of gold shimmers under their feet. The trees are majestic, and the flowers burst with colors they have never seen.

The colors of Heaven do not come in a Crayola box. It's like they've all been reinvented.

There is a sweet aroma and a joyful sound. Alternately they feel a cool breeze and warmth. The environment is perfect, and comfortable.

Everyone they encounter has a glowing countenance. Each person they meet is physically perfect. All are in perfect health, but they are all unique. The people are actively playing, working, and relaxing. All the while they worship and praise Jehovah because they are now in spirit form with their perfect bodies. It emanates from them.

Both Donovan and Wade comment to each other how there is fullness, completeness that they have never felt before. The sense of longing that every man has inside of him is now gone. The idea of worry or anxiousness is fading quickly from their spirits.

Their only desire is to be with Jesus and go to the Father.

Chapter Nine

UTTER DARKNESS

"Then the king said to his aides, 'Bind his
hands and feet and throw him into the outer
darkness, where there will be weeping and
gnashing of teeth.'"
(Matthew 22:13)

"How is it the two of us have arrived at this unholy
place together?" Carol asks Bianca.

They step into an open area, the darkness pushed
back by the light of the flames erupting from the
ground. As splendid as Heaven is, Hell is the infinitely
extreme opposite.

They are wearing their Earth clothes, which are
slowly disintegrating, turning to rags. The once

beautiful dresses have blood and bullet holes all over them.

There are no robes for those who reside here. It is only a matter of time until nakedness overtakes them.

They are keenly aware of the horrendous nature of where they are, and their physical bodies are the same as on earth, racked with pain from the wounds they received.

They are deteriorating. Just as Donovan and Wade are doing, they too are talking to one another and have concluded they have ended up in what appears to be Hell.

Carol exclaims to Bianca, "What the hell is happening?"

Bianca replies in a hushed whisper, "Hell is exactly right. Carol, we are dead, and we are in Hell".

"We can't be!" exclaims Carol. "I know I made some mistakes in my life, but I don't deserve to be in

Hell. It's worse than I ever imagined and getting worse with each step."

She is still rationalizing, hoping this is all a bad dream. "Do you feel that?"

"What?" asks Bianca.

"The profound sense of loss, the emptiness," says Carol. "You don't feel that? It's as if my heart is empty."

They cannot explain it, but it is not a nightmare. It is their new reality.

The further they walk, and the longer they linger, the dirtier they feel. With each step they take, they can hear a crunching sound. It is the familiar sound of cockroaches being crushed under their feet.

Pain is enveloping their bodies, penetrating to the depth of their souls. They can see that their skin is dripping off their bones.

A huge, ugly, monstrous creature approaches them, slapping them to the ground. This beast is fifteen to twenty feet tall with arms and legs as big as utility poles, and his skin is like that of a serpent. The eyes of this savage are red and bulging out of its head. As the monster shrieks, they can see the large, sharp teeth with the remains of a previous victim still clinging to them.

Bianca and Carol can't move. Carol is thinking of her family, her husband Sam and daughter Suzie, the great job she had, and the vacation they were planning. Sadness and dread overwhelm her to the point that she cannot pick herself up off the ground, which is now burning beneath her.

The sulfuric stench is becoming increasingly more unbearable. The heat is relentless. Rotten eggs, dead animals, and feces, the smell of these combined cannot begin to describe the putrid smell invading their senses. This is just another of the seemingly infinite torments experienced in Hell.

Carol and Bianca are somehow able to slip away. They see a number of figures, all unrecognizable to the eye because they are distorted by the effects of the fire, the worms, the maggots, and the beatings from the demons. They are able to somehow know who certain figures are.

A lost soul and a demon begin to explain what has happened and what will continue to happen without relief. "This is not the normal indoctrination for newcomers to Hell," they say.

Without any further explanation, Carol and Bianca understand that the normal indoctrination to Hell is complete and utter isolation. They sense that a human being damned to Hell will never have the blessing of a relationship with any other human being. They'll experience eternal isolation, complete separation from God and from humanity. Their only contact will be with the demons that reside there.

When a human being dies without Jesus, the soul will be instantly thrust into the torment of Hell. Because time after death is not the same as on Earth, the torment seems to happen immediately, but the soul does not escape one final encounter with Jesus.

A soul is only cast into Hell at the words of Christ, the One who shed His blood so that no one should perish in the burning fires of Hell. It is separation from God for all eternity.

Sadly, for the Father, the Son, and the Holy Spirit, not every soul is obedient in acknowledging their sin and their need for a Savior.

For a brief time, Bianca and Carol will have the knowledge of some of the lost souls they encounter. They are informed there is no escape. The judgment has been set.

The tormented soul explains the emptiness they feel is the separation from the Creator God.

Carol and Bianca cry out in anguish, "God, where are you? Help us please. We can't bear this. Lord, we will change. We'll be different. We'll live for You if You'll rescue us."

The demons laugh at them. "There is no escape from this place," they say, drool running out of their mouths.

They are told that soon they will be totally alone, not conscious of any soul around them, but they will have full memory of their lives and loved ones, all the pleasures of Earth, which will only add to their torment and pain.

As they walk, Bianca says, "What are we going to do? How did this happen to us?"

Before Carol can answer, one of the lost souls speaks out. "You failed to acknowledge the Son," he says.

Immediately, Carol and Bianca identify the soul and exclaim in unison, "You are Adolf Hitler."

"That is correct," Hitler replies. He is a shell of the person they remember from pictures in their history books, barely recognizable. His face is vacant, without life.

Their anonymous guide implores, "Keep up. It will be worse if you don't."

Adolf Hitler is only the first of several lost souls they encounter.

The next soul they meet is considered the most prolific serial killer in history. Elizabeth Bathory is said to have killed at least six hundred and fifty people several hundred years earlier.

As they continue, Bianca and Carol encounter Josef Mengele, the infamous Nazi doctor who perpetrated evil and horrible things against the Jews during the Holocaust. They also see Queen Mary I, also known as "Bloody Mary." She doesn't appear so regal now, nor does the fifth emperor of Rome, Nero. While Mengele brutalized the Jews, Nero was using Christians as human torches. The tables have surely turned.

The surprise comes when they recognize Paula Deal. Paula was one of the nicest people they knew. She passed away about six months ago. It was quite a shock to all of their friends. How could she be here? While she was not a "church person," her funeral was at the Lutheran church on Seventh Avenue. Paula was generous to a fault, always looking after children and those down on their luck. She volunteered at the soup kitchen and was always gathering used clothes for the homeless.

Paula explains her dilemma, "I loved being known as a good person, being recognized for all the charitable work I did. Almost everyone said I was a good person, a humble person, but I loved taking credit for everything I did. It is good to do good things for people, to be good to people. I know now that my motives for being good were self-serving, and I didn't admit my need for a Savior.

"I could never do enough good or be good enough to get into Heaven. Jesus is the only way. I failed to acknowledge that I was a sinner in need of a Savior. I failed to accept Jesus as the only One who could truly redeem my life. I took the credit, and I stole His glory. I worked and worked, never considering the truth of God's Word that works don't get you into Heaven. Only faith in Jesus Christ does. Now here I am.

"The real pain, the real suffering is that I no longer feel His presence. It is excruciating. While I was on

Earth, I knew of Jesus Christ. I knew Christmas was the celebration of God coming to Earth. I knew Easter was more than baskets, candy, and egg hunts. It is Easter that celebrates the blood Jesus shed on the cross, his death, and his resurrection. Yet I refused to acknowledge the One who delivers man from this place of discord and death."

Carol and Bianca met many other souls who were not guilty of murder, rape, abuse, or any of the actions and behaviors most consider so vile and evil. These souls had lived lives where they were productive for their families and humanity. They had done good things, were respected in their communities, and considered to be nice people. They went to church, to the temple, or to the mosque. These were men and women who had all failed to acknowledge that despite their "goodness," they needed a Savior because they could never be good enough in their own power to get into Heaven.

Chapter Ten

PEACE ON EARTH

"I am the Living One; I was dead, and now
look, I am alive for ever and ever! And I hold
the keys of death and Hades."
(Revelation 1:18)

In another moment in time, the salvation of mankind comes to Earth. He does not fall from the heavens above but arrives in the form of a baby.

God is never taken by surprise, He is never without a plan, and His love for mankind knows no bounds. God restored goodwill between mankind and Himself by sending His One and only Son to pay the penalty for the rebellion of Adam and Eve.

Rebellion may seem to be a strong word, but it is accurate. Any time we fail to obey God, we are rebelling against Him.

God did not have to allow Satan to rule the world. He could have easily snatched the "keys" back from him.

Yahweh is just. While it would take time to fulfill His plan, He would bring His creation back to Himself legally.

Mankind would need a lot of help to bridge the gap between them and God. They would need a sacrifice big enough to take care of the cost of their sin. The penalty that needed to be paid would have to be paid to God and to no one else.

The only thing that would suffice is a blood sacrifice of a perfect, unblemished lamb. The nation of Israel was given the chance to do it themselves by keeping the Law of Moses. As they found out, keeping the Law was impossible, and therefore many realized the need for a Savior and His saving grace. Some are still waiting for the Messiah.

The Savior was provided by God Himself. He gave His One and only Son, Jesus Christ of Nazareth.

Chapter Eleven

THE WHEAT AND
THE TARES

"To know him as he is, is to
come home."
(John Eldredge in Beautiful Outlaw)

Part I – The Judgment

On the initial journey into eternity, all dead men,
women, and children step into a beautiful room.
Donovan and Wade have stepped in to this room.
There is a single line moving toward a figure on a
seat, not a throne. He has a book in front of Him. He
does not glance at the book, as He knows exactly
what is written in it. The reactions to this figure are
vastly different.

As men and women approach the figure, you can tell there is an extreme reaction to what is taking place and to what is being said. Some people move to the right, now guided by angels. They disappear into an ethereal fog.

The others depart into a darkened hallway on the figure's left. They are alone, and you can hear screaming coming from the dark hallway, a virtual cacophony of horror. It is now clear the figure on the seat is Jesus of Nazareth.

Every person experiencing death must face Jesus. He is passing judgment on every person just as the Bible says.

Jesus is welcoming many, while others are sent away. "Depart from me, I do not know you," are Jesus' words to those who are lost. It was too late for repentance, even though they begged with bitter tears.

He tells these people He does not recognize them, even though they all recognize Him. Those He acknowledges either fall face down before Him, sobbing and exalting His name, or they fall to their knees and shout, "Hallelujah!"

Those who had a more intimate relationship with Him on Earth hug Him and praise His name. He is no stranger to them, and they are not strangers to Him. Jesus calls them His friends.

Instinctively, every person who approaches Jesus kneels before Him and speaks the words, "LORD JESUS."

Donovan begins to wonder what those men who spit on Him during his trial thought when they saw Jesus after their own deaths. What did those who mocked Him think at the moment they stood before Him?

What about those who said to Him while He hung on the cross, "Save yourself if you are the Son of God"?

What did the men who hit Him with their fists, whipped Him, and pressed a crown of thorns on His head think at this moment?

How about the man who actually nailed His hands and feet to the cross? What were his thoughts as he approached the Messiah?

Donovan's eyes met Wade's, and they again experience the same emotion at the exact same moment...unspeakable joy. This is the joy that comes in knowing the Savior Jesus Christ.

As Donovan stood before Him, Jesus spoke these words to him: "You are the righteousness of God, Donovan. I have made you righteous, and I welcome you."

Wade was given a similar greeting, and their angelic guides glowed as they took them to where they met their family and friends inside the pearl gate.

Donovan asked Wade, "Did you see the smile on our Lord's face?"

"Yes," Wade replied. "His joy at our presence was so wonderful."

Part II - Wailing

For what seemed to be a brief period of time, Bianca and Carol were separated.

Carol was in that beautiful room. She did kneel before Jesus, and she was given the dreaded command to depart from the King of all kings down the pitch-black hallway. The countenance of the Lord's face was not of anger, but sorrow.

During that time, Bianca also met Jesus but not in the room of judgment. As she reflects on what just happened, she thinks, *I cannot truly describe the feelings I had in His presence. Love radiated from Him as well as kindness, gentleness, and everything Carol and I were not experiencing in the darkness. He never spoke. He was just present in absolute glory.*

Carol and Bianca are reunited and continue to proceed into the darkness.

"Where were you?" Carol asks.

"I met Him," Bianca says.

"Who?" asks Carol.

"Jesus," says Bianca. "He didn't say anything, but He was with me."

"I met Him too," Carol responded. "But He did not acknowledge my presence, and I was told to depart."

The darkness enveloping those who pass down this tunnel is like an all-consuming fire. The demons – fallen angels and misguided followers of Lucifer – torment the souls who come through. These demons are sadistic and angry as they too have an astute understanding of what will ultimately happen to them as a result of their foolish choices.

These humans are like playthings, rag dolls and punching bags used to vent their evil vindictiveness on. These battered souls are writhing on the filthy ground, crawling away as quickly as they can in an effort to hide.

It's as if the demons of Hell have been outfitted with night-vision goggles. They easily retrieve the lost souls and continue to pummel them.

As people enter the darkness, you can hear the wailing and gnashing of teeth. It is just as the Word says it will be. These people have an acute awareness of their lives, their families, and the huge error they made in not acknowledging Jesus as the Son of God while they were alive. They are now trying to grip the realization that they no longer have any hope. They angrily rationalize and justify their failure to acknowledge Him. Their only hope was Jesus, and they refused Him. Now the emptiness begins to consume them. There is not even the faintest hint of Jesus any longer. The judgment is set.

Carol asks, "Why did Jesus come to you and not to me? Why did I have to depart from His presence? I have heard about Him all my life. Christmas and Easter, you know how it is. I was just too busy for church and the hypocrites that inhabit that place."

Bianca replies, "I don't know why He appeared to me. It doesn't make any sense, especially since we are here in Hell. From what I do know, He doesn't hang around this place much. The Father is here. He is omnipresent, but no one feels His presence or His Holiness."

Part III – Pure Joy

Those guided by the angels are either extremely animated as they shout for joy or so overcome by the awesomeness of Christ that the angels have to carry them into the beautiful city. This is where Donovan and Wade arrive.

Wade thinks, *This city is so utterly delightful to all of the senses. I'm overwhelmed by the beauty, the fragrances, and the sounds. Everything is so bright, not in a blinding way, but in a way that sparkles in its completeness. There aren't enough adjectives to describe what I'm seeing, and the ones I know are so insufficient to do the job.*

The angelic guides assure everyone they will become accustomed to this incredible place.

There are so many different kinds of trees. Some are tall, some are short, but all have magnificent full canopies. The carpet-like grass is so green and plush. Exotic does not begin to describe the beauty of the flowers or their infinite variety.

Beautiful buildings blend seamlessly into the landscape. There are no shadows or darkness of any kind. It is absolutely incredible.

In the distance you can see majestic mountains. You know they are far away, and yet you feel like you could reach out and touch them. It's like watching a 3D movie.

There is also a mesmerizing area in the distance. You are automatically drawn to it. It is the Sanctuary of Yahweh, the throne room of El Shaddai, God Almighty. There are flashes of lightning all around it, and a thunderous sound emanates from that direction. It is not the same as the thunder on Earth, but voices shouting, "HOLY, HOLY, HOLY" resonate from it, and the reverberation is pleasing to the ears.

There is a power in the sound, and yet it is not overpowering to the ears. It fills everyone with peace, strength, and love.

All is at rest in this place. It is the fullness of Christ.

Yes, this is Heaven. The guides tell Wade he is looking at the dwelling place of the Creator.

While God is omnipresent, this is the place that scripture describes as the throne of God. This is the very place from which He reigns. It is His Holy Sanctuary.

As Wade walks down the main street, it is in fact gold. Not all of the streets are gold. Some are silver. Others are made from jasper, sapphire, emerald, onyx, carnelian, and other precious stones.

He can hear children playing, and people are moving about the streets. Wade and Donovan are on the way to I AM's throne. They pass by the most incredible garden they've ever seen.

The angel says, "This is the Garden of Eden."

Wade is invited to look inside. There are no longer guards as there is no longer a need for them. Jesus has settled all accounts.

There are incredible houses. If the Taj Mahal is the standard for beauty back on Earth, it is a run-down shack in comparison to these mansions.

The walls seen in Heaven are not needed for the protection of anything. Unlike in the Garden of Eden where the serpent lurked, there are no such dangers here. No danger. No death. The war is over! Lord Jesus is the victorious King!

Nothing here has a flaw or blemish. Everything is so very perfect. Sin is not a part of Heaven, and there is no temptation.

With love from the Father comes love for the Father. While there are many, many people, there is also plenty of space, and nothing seems crowded. A lot is here, and yet everything seems to be easily accessible.

While Wade does not feel hungry or thirsty, he desires a drink and food. The water flowing from the fountains everywhere is so satisfying. That water comes from the River of Life, a clear, crystal river flowing from the throne of God.

As Wade drinks the water, it seems to run all the way through his body. He is given a piece of bread. The smell is marvelous, and the taste is indescribable. It literally melts in his mouth.

The roads run next to lakes, and the water is like glass, calm, crystal, transparent. The rivers are the most incredible blues and greens yet clear so you can see fish and other gorgeous, aquatic creatures and plants.

There is nothing boring about this place. Men and women in Heaven are not floating on clouds, playing harps. Nor are all the people gathered together chanting to the Father.

This is a place of activity. This is a place of joy and fun. It is a place of celebration. Boredom is not a part of Heaven.

Whenever a new soul arrives, Heaven erupts in joyous cheers of HALLELUJAH!

Chapter Twelve

In the Father's Presence

"… Holy, holy, holy,
is the Lord God, the Almighty …"
(Revelation 4:8)

Donovan and Wade are captivated by the wonders of Heaven. It is all so magnificent. They have come to this place together, and their thoughts again blend as they begin the journey to the Father's house. There is no talking between them, only the synchronized viewing of the images they are seeing.

The street of gold is the pathway taken to the Throne of God. No doubt a little of this revelation takes place in the *Wizard of Oz*. There are so many places on Earth where God reveals Himself and His majesty. The yellow brick road is just yellow bricks, and the Emerald City is no match for the Kingdom of Heaven.

The throne room of God just cannot be described. Even John's attempt to describe it in the Book of Revelation is insufficient.

The reality of these men's experience is beyond the words of any human. At one point, they speak with John, who was apologetic with regard to his inadequate description of Heaven.

John told Donovan and Wade that his life on earth with Jesus had been so filled with wonder. When Jesus spoke to him on the island of Patmos, he was "blown away" by what had been revealed to him. The two men chuckle at John's use of this colloquial expression. John winks and laughs as he watches the two men's faces while he continues to recount the descriptions given in Revelation.

As they draw closer, they can see that the true Temple of God, the absolute Holy of Holies, is an immense structure. It seems to have no boundaries, to be infinite, and yet it is intimate and not overwhelming.

John painted his portrait of Heaven based on what he knew and could relate to from his time on earth. Wade and Donovan contemplate the difficulty they would have describing this indescribable place. They can feel the presence of God, and His LOVE caresses their spirits.

Hebrews 8:2 comes to their minds. "Elohim resides in the heavenly tabernacle, the true place of worship built by the LORD and not by human hands."

They remember John's writing from Revelation 4: 3-6a, "The One sitting on the throne was as brilliant as gemstones – like beryl and amethyst. An emerald glow encircles His throne like a rainbow.

"Twenty-four thrones surround him, and twenty-four elders are seated in them. They are all clothed in white and have gold crowns on their heads.

"From the throne come flashes of lightning, and the rumble of thunder. In front of the throne is a shiny sea of glass, sparkling like crystal."

Jesus appears next to Wade and takes him by the hand. He can feel that his hands are tender and strong. He reaches out and pats Donovan gently on the shoulder. He says to them, "The Father delights to be with you and speak to you."

The men's knees buckle, but the Son easily holds them up. They are going into the presence of the Almighty…The Great I AM.

Jesus guides Donovan and Wade down a long hallway with curtains of finely woven linen. They are decorated with blue, purple, and scarlet thread and with skillfully embroidered cherubim. There are gold and brass clasps holding them in place and silver bases at the bottom.

They enter into a large, cavernous room, and the floor is sapphire stone. Angels are moving about, their movements fluid and effortless. These breathtaking creatures are radiant in their silky raiment.

Jesus points out both Michael and Gabriel, who appear to be at least fifteen feet tall. They are also radiant and exude strength and confidence.

Donovan and Wade have a difficult time comprehending these two magnificent creatures. Jesus reminds the men that the way these angels appear to their eyes is for the benefit of man's comprehension. He says, "You need a point of reference because their physical appearances are not their true forms." He then reminds them that just as He appears in human form, He is still God.

A vast crowd is present, its number too many to count. They appear to be from every nation, tribe, and tongue on earth. They are standing in front of the throne of Jesus, the Lamb of God, clothed in white robes and holding palm branches in their hands. They shout, "Salvation comes from our God who sits on the throne and from the Lamb!"

Both men are uncertain how they have not exploded or melted or something. As they pass by the two archangels, they hear them whisper to them, "Fear not."

"Easy for them to say, they've been here forever," Donovan and Wade say in unison, speaking out loud for the first time since they began the trip to the Throne of God.

Jesus reminds them that because of Him, they can step boldly into the presence of the Father. As they do, they try to remember the whole "come boldly" thing, but instead, they stretch out on the floor face down in front of Yahweh.

It is as the Bible describes it. He is sitting on the throne and is as brilliant as gemstones – like jasper and carnelian. The glow of an emerald circles His throne like a rainbow, and the delightful smell of incense sifts through the air from a golden censer.

Wade and Donovan are reminded of what Isaiah 6:1-5 says in the Bible: "In the year that King Uzziah died, I saw also the LORD sitting upon a throne, high and lifted up, and his train filled the temple. Above it stood the seraphim: each one had six wings; with twain he covered his face, and with twain he covered his feet, and with twain he did fly. And one cried unto another, and said, holy, holy, holy, is the LORD of hosts: the whole earth is full of his glory. And the posts of the door moved at the voice of him that cried, and the house was filled with smoke. Then they said, 'I, Woe is me! for I am undone; because I am a man of unclean lips, and I dwell in the midst of a people of unclean lips; for mine eyes have seen the King, the LORD of hosts.'"

Wade and Donovan feel they can't remain present because His Holiness is so great. He is absolutely pure and complex.

The joy and peace that runs through them is beyond their understanding. Harkening back to the Cowardly Lion in *The Wizard of Oz*, they might have run, but they couldn't move. Forget speaking; they were like puddles of water on the floor.

Again, Jesus gently picks the two of them up and assures them of God's love. Jesus says, "There's something the Father would like to ask you."

Donovan remembers all the times this happened to him on earth. He would feel something in his spirit questioning what he was going to do in a particular situation. He remembers it's not because Jehovah is clueless; it's His way of helping His children come into agreement with Him.

"Come up here," the Father says to them in a voice that is gentle and sweet. "Do you like it here?"

While they can't see His face, they sense He's having some fun with them. The smile on Jesus' face gives them a clue. They feel the Father's and Son's love and begin to relax a little.

The next question is a lot more serious. "Do you want to stay, or would you like to return to your lives on Earth? Both of you have pleased Me with the gift of life that I gave to you. You both are men who have made an impact for My Kingdom and brought Me glory.

"Wade, your healing and this experience will give you an opportunity to testify to My greatness in a way that others have not been able to. The time is drawing near for Me to take My Church and for My Son to return. The desire of My heart is to bring all of the remaining souls home to Me."

Wade responds, "Gracious Heavenly Father, I cannot imagine leaving You now. How can I ever be the same? How can I not be empty on Earth knowing and experiencing everything here with You?"

God replies, "You have experienced My presence on Earth. When you return, you will have a much greater understanding of My being present with you. This is part of your mission. You are to help others walk in the Spirit so there will be an outpouring of My presence, which will in turn draw men to Me as never before. The time is near for My Son to return. You must convey the urgency of My message. My beloved Son will be there soon!"

Donovan asks, "And what about me, Lord? What shall I do?"

"Donovan, your work is complete," God responds. "You have completed all that I had for you. Each of My children's time is in My hands. All are given the opportunity to join Me in My work. Some choose not to join Me, but you did, and through the power of My beloved Son, you have overcome many enemies and obstacles. You are now secure in your Father's bosom. Welcome home!"

"I am glad to stay. Thank you, Father," says Donovan.

Wade inquires, "LORD, how can I return to Earth if Donovan doesn't? I'll be sad, and I'll miss him. He has been such a big part of my life."

God replies, "Everyone on Earth feels the loss of loved ones. I created you to feel that way. I feel that way when My creation rejects Me. You are made for relationship, first with Me and then with each other.

"Donovan has been a big part of your life because that was My desire for the two of you. He is not your life. I AM your life.

"Wade, you will be able to bring a comfort to Donovan's family in their loss that no one else can bring. You will be able to assure them that he is with Me and that they will see him again one day.

"The same Spirit that raised My Son is in you. He will be your strength."

"I want to remain with you, Father, but I will do as You have asked," Wade responds.

Chapter Thirteen

SEPARATION AND A SECOND CHANCE

"But God shows his love for us in that
while we were still sinners, Christ died for us."
(Romans 5:8)

"Bianca, I can't move," moans Carol. "It feels like I'm paralyzed. The beating we're taking, being tossed about and thrown up against these grimy walls, the dust, the filth, the smell, and the pain are too much for me to bear, but it doesn't stop. Can't you help me?"

Bianca responds in a weak voice, "I'm empty. I have nothing, and my feeling of hopelessness is overwhelming. We are doomed."

Carol is lifted high over the head of a horrific-looking demon. Its face is contorted so drastically that there is no symmetry in it. His eyes are yellow and red. One is set higher than the other. The pointed ears are misshapen, perhaps from skirmishes with other demons. His mouth is full of razor-sharp teeth and a tongue that is long and forked. The snorts from the grossly deformed nose are loud and laborious.

He is at least fifteen feet tall. His arms and legs are as thick as oil drums. He is covered with scales similar to an alligator's skin, and his hands and feet have six digits with claws like knives.

These claws rip what's left of Carol's skin as she is being raised up and thrown down again and again. She cries out in terror and pain. Flapping his bat-like wings, the demon picks her up and then rises off the filthy earth. He then tosses her into a dark pit that appears to be bottomless. Her sorrowful screams eventually fade. She is lost forever.

As Bianca manages to roll over, she sees a different figure. She can't see much other than a hand reaching down to take hold of hers. The figure helps her to her feet and props her up on his hip. She recognizes him. It's Jesus.

What is he doing here? she wonders.

As He begins to speak to Bianca, the expression on His face is gentle, and His eyes have a kindness she has never seen in anyone.

He tells her that He has come for her. As He speaks to her, there is no harshness in his voice, no judgment in his tone.

He says, "I am the Messiah, the Son of God. I am the Savior of all mankind. You did not believe in Me, but your time of judgment has not come. Sam's bullets ended Carol's life but they did not end your life. You are not yet subject to the Judgment.

"Yes, you attended church. You sang in the choir, you went to Sunday school, and you were even baptized, but you never gave your heart to

Me. You have become aware of and experienced the discord of Hell, but your time on earth is not finished.

"You will be returning to Earth and to your family. You are to acknowledge Me and share this experience. You must make the most of this opportunity, for the glory of God and His Kingdom. I will soon be returning for My Bride. Do you understand?"

"Yes, Lord, I do, and I acknowledge You as my Savior," Bianca responds in a barely audible whisper. "Thank you, oh, thank you, thank you!"

Her body is bowed low, her face to the ground. "What about Carol? What has happened to Carol?" Bianca asks.

"The judgment is set for her," Jesus replies. The sadness in His voice and on His face is evident. "Remember this as you testify to what you have seen.

The Father will be sending Me soon. He is telling you to get them ready.

"This is not a new message," He concludes.

Chapter Fourteen

RETURN TO EARTH

"And they have defeated him by the blood of
the Lamb and by their testimony; …"
(Revelation 12:11)

Part I – Healed

When Wade opens his eyes, he is no longer in the room he was in at the time of the attack. That room and most of Baptist Hospital have been destroyed. He is now at Northside Hospital. A nurse is attending to him.

Outside Wade's room are several firemen and EMTs talking about what has happened at Baptist Hospital.

Wade stands up. He is disoriented. "Where are my wife and children? Where is Donovan?" His faced is wrinkled with concern.

The nurse replies, "Your family is safe. They were downstairs in an area of the hospital that wasn't hit by the attack. They got out of the building before any real damage happened. I'm sorry, but your friend was not so lucky. He died from the injuries he received."

"No, he's not dead! He can't be dead! I was just with him. We were in Heaven," exclaims Wade.

The transition back to Earth confuses Wade. He is still trying to decipher whether his experience in Heaven was real, a dream, or a hallucination caused by the medication.

The nurse looks sympathetically at him and says, "They have taken his body to the hospital morgue, but his spirit may very well be in Heaven."

Then he realizes it wasn't a dream. He really was in Heaven. He remembers the Father's promise to him, and a peaceful smile encompasses his face. "Yes, it is. He is with Jesus," Wade says joyously.

Wade stands, now dressed in his clothes, alive and strong. His wounds are superficial. He has only scrapes, scratches, and some bruises. The nurse has not fully understood what has happened as the result of the terrorist attack. She is confused by Wade's generally healthy condition when hundreds of others were killed or seriously injured.

This attack is being compared to the horrific attack on the Heartbeat Night Club. Somehow Orlando has become the focus of terror rather than the happiness and fun of the theme parks. The man she is talking to is alive and healthy, yet moments ago he was on the verge of death.

Wade's mind is spinning. The sickness, the bombing, the visit to Heaven, it doesn't make any sense.

He looks at a clock on the wall. "How long has it been since all of this started?"

The nurse glances at the clock on the wall. "About fifty minutes have passed since the first missile hit the hospital room where you and Donovan were."

God's time and Earth time are entirely different, and this only adds to Wade's confusion.

Emily and the girls are waiting for Wade in a room down the hallway. The nurse asks Wade to have a seat in a wheelchair, even though it is obviously not needed. He does not refuse and plops down in the seat. The nurse then rolls him down the hallway to a most delightful reunion with his wife and children.

Wade stands up, and Emily and the girls look up with astonished expressions. They all squeal in delight.

Emily shouts, "It's a miracle! It's a miracle! Wade, you are alive and walking! How can this be?"

Wade holds out his arms, and Emily, Layla, and Sophia collapse in them, crying with joy.

He says to Emily, "We have a lot to talk about. We have a lot to do. He is coming, and we have to let everyone know to get ready. They have to get ready now!"

Emily replies, "Who is coming?"

Wade says, "Jesus is! I have been to Heaven! I have met the Father!"

Several nurses, who overhear the conversation, join Emily in an effort to calm Wade down. He is moving around the room with his hands raised over his head. He is jumping up and down enthusiastically and incoherently talking about the mission he has received from God. They assume he has suffered a brain injury and is delusional.

"I'm not crazy, Em!" he exclaims. "I have...WE HAVE a very important job to do. Jesus is coming, and the sooner He comes, the sooner I can go back to Heaven where I truly belong, where WE truly belong!"

Emily replies, "Okay, Wade, you can tell us more about it later. Right now, you need to calm down so that we can make sure you're okay, and we can get out of here."

In the days and weeks after the terrorist attack on the hospital, Wade and Emily often take walks in their neighborhood and surrounding parks. Wade can remember walking through the perfection of Heaven, but it does not diminish his current walks in this fallen world. He is here with the love of his life, sharing what he experienced in Heaven. He knows he will help others make Heaven their final destination as well. While Earth is beautiful, it is nothing compared to Heaven.

He observes the imperfections in his surroundings with a new appreciation. The cracked sidewalks need to be pressure washed. The grass is so wonderfully green, but there are always areas where it is thinner, worn by people walking on it or where animals have dug it up. The trees are beautiful as well, but the bark on the trunks just can't match what he saw in Heaven. These trees suffer from broken branches and brown leaves. Yet nothing is dead or worn in Heaven.

"It's all so perfect in Heaven," Wade tells Emily. "I can't wait to go back. I can't wait to show you all its wonders!" he exclaims, his face radiating joy.

He struggles with his longing for his true home; he is homesick.

Part II – A New Life

Bianca opens her eyes and sees nurses and a doctor hovering over her. They seem surprised that she has opened her eyes.

She tries to get up. It has been three days since the shooting.

The doctor tells her not to move. The serious tone of his voice convinces her to be still.

Her injuries are very serious, and her recovery is going to take weeks, if not months or even years. Bianca now sees Marcos out of the corner of her eye and manages a weak smile.

The doctor says, "You have been through a lot. You are lucky to be alive. For the first twenty-four hours, we didn't think you were going to make it, and then your body began to respond positively."

As the doctor exits, one of the nurses tells her that she was shot up pretty bad, but the bullets didn't hit any vital organs. The most serious concern was the loss of blood.

"Blood," she mumbles to herself. "Blood gives life. Jesus shed His blood to give me life."

She remembers the mission Jesus gave to her. She realizes her recovery is going to surprise everyone.

Marcos stands up, tears streaming from his eyes. He is visibly shaken by her appearance yet relieved she is alive. She starts to explain what happened. Marcos stops her.

"Shhh, I know what happened. The police told me," says Marcos. "You tried to save her. You were willing to sacrifice your life for hers. You are so brave, so incredibly brave."

"I'm not talking about the shooting. Marcos, I was in Hell, and I wasn't brave there. It was so horrible and terrifying!

"I can't wait to get out of this hospital. I am grateful to be okay and for all the work the doctors and nurses are doing for me, but I feel so closed in. My cell in Hell was so dark, and the walls seemed to always be pressing in on me.

"I just want to see the sun and the trees. I want to walk barefoot in the grass and feel the breeze on my face," Bianca says.

She whispers, "Marcos, Jesus has given me a mission, and I want to share that mission with you."

"Whatever you want," he replies. "You can tell me more after you get well."

"It was so incredible. Carol and I got a glimpse of Heaven, but the experience of Hell was so awful," she says, shaking with fear as some of those scenes flash through her mind.

"You have to calm down. Everything is going to be all right," Marcos assures her. "We're together now."

Chapter Fifteen

"Yes, I Am coming soon!"

"… Amen! Come, Lord Jesus!"
(Revelation 22:20b)

A year passes.

Wade and Bianca are healthy and whole. Wade has no cancer, It is not in remission; it is totally gone as if it had never been there. It has been gone since the moment of the attack on the hospital.

There are also no physical or psychological effects from the attack. Wade's beautiful coffee complexion has returned, and he is back to the strong and handsome man he was prior to cancer's attack on him.

Bianca's wounds healed much faster than the medical team anticipated. They have no explanation. The physical scars remain.

She has virtually no memory of the shooting, but she remembers Carol and her experiences of Hell. Bianca has forgiven Sam and married Marcos. Bianca Vega is now Bianca Bravo, and she has just discovered that she is pregnant. The Lord's favor continues to rain down on her.

Marcos and Bianca moved to Orlando, Florida, and now attend Southland Church where she met Wade, Emily, and their girls.

As they have shared their testimonies with others, the LORD brought them together to speak as a team. Their message is not new, but it is more urgent than ever before. Time is running out! There is only one way back to our Father in Heaven, and that one way is Jesus Christ the Nazarene.

Wade describes the magnificence of Heaven and how we should all be looking forward with great excitement to going to our eternal home to be with Jesus. He talks about his best friend Donovan and the peace and joy they shared in Heaven.

Wade tries to explain the longing he has to be in Heaven with Jesus and how he misses Donovan. He is literally homesick for Heaven.

While he does miss Donovan, he rejoices in knowing exactly where his best friend is and that he will see him again.

God has kept His promise to Wade in the peace (Shalom) he feels each day as he is led by the Holy Spirit. His desire to return to Heaven, his homesickness, is always relieved by the reception of his story as he tells it to others. Tens of thousands have chosen a life with Christ from simply hearing his testimony. By choosing Christ, they have chosen Heaven.

Bianca testifies to the flipside of eternity, the horrors of Hell, and the great pain in being separated from God the Father. While we are all God's creation, only those who acknowledge Jesus Christ as Lord and Savior are God's children, joint heirs with His Son.

Bianca spells it out very clearly what is in store for those who reject Jesus. She should know. She was there; she met lost souls and watched as the friend she loved perished into the darkness.

No one would be homesick for Hell. Even the devil himself is fearful of his eternal fate. Unlike Adam and Eve, who were once banished from the Garden of Eden but are now present with God in Heaven, Satan will never reside again in the presence of God.

Wade and Bianca have teamed up to share their testimonies of God's goodness and love and the message of urgency regarding Jesus' return. Love is the answer.

The Word tells us that God is love in 1 John 4:8. Wade and Bianca tell us He is coming soon, so now is the time to believe and receive.

Since Adam and Eve were exiled from the Garden of Eden, all of creation has awaited the Redeemer, the

Promised One who can restore order to the chaos of the fallen world. He came over two thousand years ago, and His name is Jesus. This is the Gospel. This is the good news.

It is now all Christians' privilege to tell everyone about Him, to introduce our families, our friends, and our neighbors to Him. Non-believers think they know what is coming, what is going to happen, but they don't really know. Christians do.

All Christians have an incredible story to tell and a personal testimony to give. The Lord has warned us that many would continue to reject His message and their testimonies.

Epilogue

Rapture and Tribulation

"Then, together with them, we who are still
alive and remain on the earth will be caught up
in the clouds to meet the Lord in the air. ..."
(1 Thessalonians 4:17a)

"For then there will be great tribulation, such
as has not been from the beginning of the
world until now, no, and never will be."
(Matthew 24:21)

Eighteen months after Wade and Bianca return to Earth, Jesus comes for the Church. They have been diligent in their effort to tell the world that the time of the Lord's return is imminent, and now He has taken His Bride from the earth.

Wade and Bianca have shared their testimonies across the globe, resulting in hundreds of thousands of people receiving Jesus as their personal Savior. At one evangelic event, over three thousand men and women came forward after hearing Wade's experience in Heaven. It was just like Pentecost.

His message is one of hope. He would tell people not to just fear Hell but to embrace the love of the Father in Heaven. Many commented afterward that his description of Heaven was so vivid and his experience in meeting with God so believable, they could not hold themselves from coming forward to profess their newfound faith in Jesus Christ.

At another event, Bianca experienced a similar outpouring of acceptance of her story as hundreds made their way to the altar. She was in the unique position of testifying to the terrors of Hell. She agreed with Wade's testimony to allow Jesus to embrace each of them in the way He has embraced her.

Men and women were overheard as they sobbed with tears of joy, saying that Bianca's testimony of her encounter with Jesus removed any doubt they had of God's love for them and how just and righteous He is. Wade and Bianca pleaded with those who refused to accept the urgency of making a decision for Christ because they knew time was running out, and now it has.

It is just as it has been described in the Bible, where millions of people have vanished from the earth. The speculative descriptions of the moment and time immediately following the rapture turn out to be accurate.

There are many planes that crash, but because of the auto-pilot program, not every plane goes down. Trains, semi-trucks, motorcycles, and cars crash by the thousands with an incredible number of fatalities. The people who die under these circumstances have no chance of salvation, while those left behind will face a very difficult decision.

The men and women left behind will have to take the mark that allows them to continue to move freely in the world or to become "runners" or fugitives of the

New World Order. Those who are fugitives invariably are confused at what is going on and yet at the same time understand what has happened.

Most of the world will accept the New World Order, knowing their mortal existence depends on it. They do not see any other practical choice.

Those who are on the run sense their eternal existence is on the line. While these people did not make their declaration for Christ in time to be included in His rapture, they are now painfully aware they will most assuredly forfeit their human existence for not accepting the mark of the beast. How long can a person possibly hide in this new reality?

Bill and Jasmine Campbell are two such people. Wade's and Bianca's testimonies have captured the attention of this young couple. The Campbells had been attending Southland regularly and seem to be close to a decision for Christ. Before they make this decision, God removes His Church from the world. It is the Rapture of the Church. It really has happened!

As the Tribulation unfolds, Bill and Jasmine are frightened and confused. They are among those described as runners or fugitives of the New World Order.

The government tries to explain away the disappearance of the millions of people in the United States and around the world, saying alien abduction is the only plausible explanation. The people who now inhabit earth eagerly accept this reasoning. Years of watching Hollywood movies and television shows about alien invasions have brainwashed people into believing the lie.

Chaos is rampant worldwide. Governments all around the world are crumbling as people try to come to grips with what has happened. While most people are in denial that God has taken His people, there are men and women like the Campbells who do understand what has happened, and more importantly, what is going to happen.

While the Holy Spirit was present on the earth, people had hope. Now with the absence of the Holy

Spirit, there is no one to convict mankind any longer of their need for a Savior.

Eternal life continues to hang in the balance. Each man and woman will be forced to make a choice. They must accept the new government's mark and live, or reject the mark and be put to death.

Those who do not accept the mark are not automatically thrust into Heaven. The acknowledgement of the Cross of Calvary and the One who was slain is still necessary.

Salvation is still possible, but it will require a martyr's death. Without the mark 666, no one is able to work or buy food and other items necessary to live.

Because of the collapse of every national government on the planet, a new world order emerges under the leadership of the charismatic Ambrose Fontaine. He is the Antichrist.

As Bill and Jasmine watch the events unfold on television, they stare into the screen in disbelief.

"This can't be happening!" they say in unison. They look at each other and again say at the same time, "What are we going to do?"

Bill's voice quivers as he asks, "Should we head to the mountains or make our way to the coast and find a boat?"

Uncertain how to respond, Jasmine says, "We have to get to the church. Maybe there will be others there who can help us figure out what to do. We can work together to survive."

Bill responds, "How will we know who we can trust?"

As the television and Internet continue to report events around the globe, people are able to see the masses gathering in major cities around the world. These reports are interrupted by the picture of a single man—Ambrose Fontaine—waiting to speak to the entire world.

The world audience is captivated by this man's speech. In light of the anarchy taking hold of the world, he appears to be calm, smiling and speaking softly, clearly, and confidently. He is not shouting or screaming. In fact, he doesn't even raise his voice.

Mr. Fontaine explains he had known for many years the present events were coming. The tone of his voice has a soothing tenor to it. He has been working on a plan to meet the demand of this time in history.

The camera pans to reveal many of the heads of state and other men and women who are leaders in their respective countries around the world. As Ambrose Fontaine outlines his plan for handling the current events and the future, these men and women nod their heads in agreement, clapping their hands in affirmation of this new leader.

All around the world, you can almost hear a collective sigh of relief and the feeling that everything is going to be okay. This is the devil's final lie.

This is not the end. While Jesus has taken His people, His Church, His Bride from this earth, the story does not end there. The battle of Armageddon ensues:

"Then I saw heaven opened and a white horse standing there; and the one sitting on the horse was named Faithful and True—the one who justly punishes and makes war. [12] His eyes were like flames, and on his head were many crowns.

A name was written on his forehead, and only he knew its meaning. [13] He was clothed with garments dipped in blood, and his title was 'The Word of God.'

[14] The armies of heaven, dressed in finest linen, white and clean, followed him on white horses. [15] In his mouth he held a sharp sword to strike down the nations; he ruled them with an iron grip; and he trod the winepress of the fierceness of the

wrath of Almighty God. [16] On his robe and thigh was written this title: 'King of Kings and Lord of Lords'" (Revelation 19: 11-16, The Living Bible).

And finally, Satan is destroyed:

"When the thousand years end, Satan will be let out of his prison. [8] He will go out to deceive the nations of the world and gather them together, with Gog and Magog, for battle—a mighty host, numberless as sand along the shore.

[9] They will go up across the broad plain of the earth and surround God's people and the beloved city of Jerusalem on every side. But fire from God in heaven will flash down on the attacking armies and consume them. [10] Then the devil who had betrayed them will again be thrown into the Lake of Fire burning with sulfur

where the Creature and False Prophet are, and they will be tormented day and night forever and ever" (Revelation 20:7-10, The Living Bible).

About the Author

FREDDIE TYLER

Freddie Tyler was born in Orlando, Florida and raised in Winter Park, Florida with his three older sisters and older brother. He is the son of E.Q. (Tim) Tyler and Audrey Waterman Tyler. He graduated high school from The Bolles School in Jacksonville, Florida in 1972. He was an outstanding swimmer, winning eight out of eight State Championships between 1968 and 1972.

Freddie competed for the United States in the 1972 Olympic Games held in Munich, West Germany, where he won a gold medal as a part of the 800-meter freestyle relay. He was also a champion swimmer for Indiana University where he graduated with a degree in business in 1977. In 1980, Freddie began a thirty-five-year teaching and coaching career at West Orange High School in Winter Garden, Florida.

Freddie married his wife Renee in October of 1980, and they have three children (Brian, Jennifer, and Bridget) and three grandchildren (Ethan, Kyla, and Cohen).

While he claims his salvation came as a young man, he acknowledges that it wasn't until December 26, 2005 that he allowed Jesus to take control of his life. At that time, he began to realize there is more to salvation than Heaven. It was time to live for Jesus here on earth.

[You can contact him on Facebook at tapintogodslove.]

CPSIA information can be obtained
at www.ICGtesting.com
Printed in the USA
BVHW03s0227260418
514392BV00020B/663/P